Can't Catch Me!

Michael Foreman

HINKLER
BOOKS

"Goodnight, Little Monkey," said Mum.
"Sweet dreams."

"No! It's too early for bed,"
said Little Monkey ...

"Can't catch ME!"

"Can't catch ME!"

"GRRRRRR!

GARRRRRROOO!

Coming to get you and when we do . . ."

"Can't catch ME!"

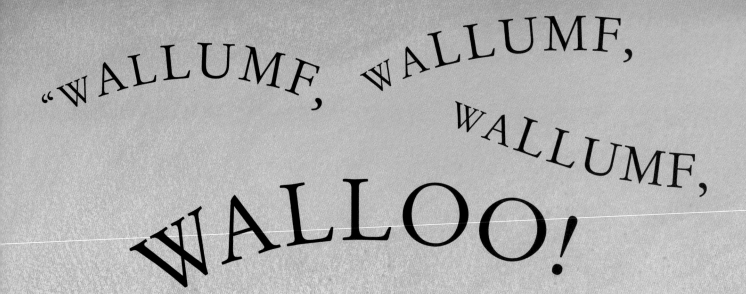

"WALLUMF, WALLUMF, WALLUMF, WALLOO!

Coming to get you and when we do . . ."

"SNAPPETTY SNAP, SNACKAROOO!
Coming to get you and when we do . . ."

"BEEP BEEP, BEEP BEEP, BEEP BEEP,

BOOO!

Coming to get you and when we do ..."

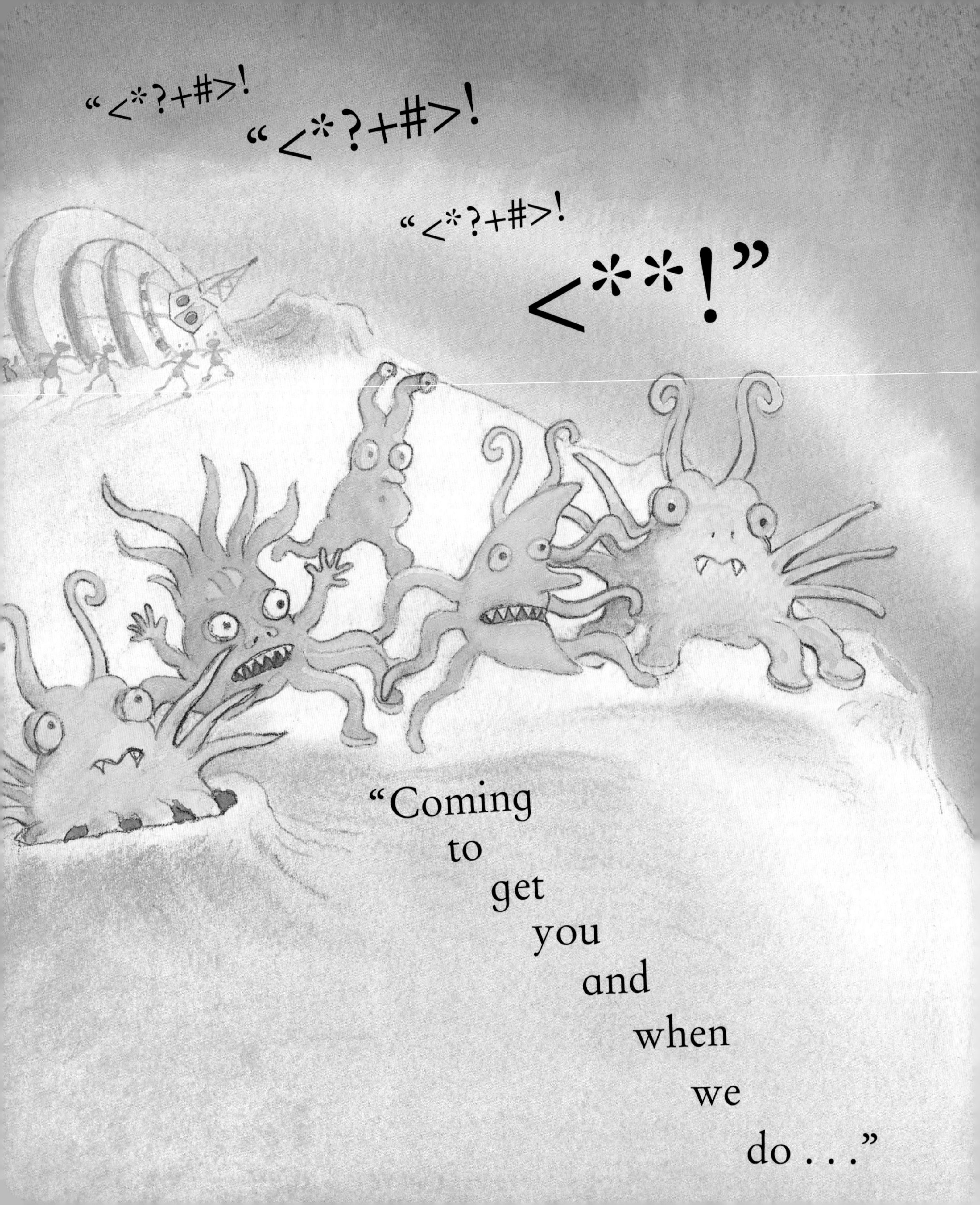

"<*?+#>!

"<*?+#>!

"<*?+#>!

<**!"

"Coming to get you and when we do . . ."

"Can't catch . . .

"HARRAH! HARROOO!

Now we'll get you —
and we're going to . . .

CAN'T CATCH . . .

"There, I've got you, safe and sound!
Come on, Little Monkey,
time for bed . . .

Good night, sleep tight.
Sweet Dreams."

Published by Hinkler Books Pty Ltd
45–55 Fairchild Street
Heatherton Victoria 3202 Australia
www.hinklerbooks.com

First published by Andersen Press Ltd., London

Text © Michael Foreman 2005
Illustrations © Michael Foreman 2005
Cover design © Hinkler Books 2010

Cover design: Peter Tovey
Prepress: Graphic Print Group

ISBN: 978 1 7418 4431 3

Printed and bound in China